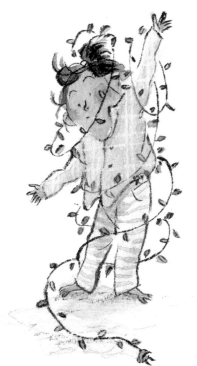

A Year of
Everyday
Wonders

words by **Cheryl B. Klein**   pictures by **Qin Leng**

Abrams Books for Young Readers • New York

For Dashiell Francis Monohan, and all your firsts to come
—C.B.K.

To Lou, may you enjoy all your firsts
—Q.L.

The illustrations in this book were made with ink and watercolor.

Cataloging-in-Publication Data has been applied for and may be obtained from the Library of Congress.

ISBN 978-1-4197-4208-8

Text copyright © 2020 Cheryl B. Klein
Illustrations copyright © 2020 Qin Leng
Book design by Steph Stilwell

Printed and bound in China
10 9 8 7 6 5 4 3 2 1

Abrams Books for Young Readers are available at special discounts when purchased in quantity for
premiums and promotions as well as fundraising or educational use. Special editions can also be created
to specification. For details, contact specialsales@abramsbooks.com or the address below.

Abrams® is a registered trademark of Harry N. Abrams, Inc.

ABRAMS The Art of Books
195 Broadway, New York, NY 10007
abramsbooks.com

First day of the new year

First wake-up

First waffles

First fight with your brother

First snowfall

First snowballs

First hot chocolate

First stories

First valentine

First cold

First crush

First new umbrella

First lost umbrella

First green in the gray

First short sleeves

First missed bus

Ninety-seventh fight
with your brother

First haircut   Second haircut

First ice-cream truck

First beach trip

First splash battle

First sunburn

First sparklers

First summer storm

Second new umbrella

First family reunion

First cousins' prank

Two hundred twenty-sixth fight with your brother

First new teacher

Second lost umbrella

Second crush

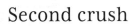

First gold in the green

First mask

Last cape

First snow day

Second snow day

Third snow day

Fourth snow day

Three hundred eighty-fourth
fight with your brother

First giving

First getting

Last wake-up

Last waffles

Last snowfall

Last stories

First day of the new year